DREAMS IN TIME

KENZIE SKYE

ONE

I slide the yellowed parchment into a protective plastic sleeve, marveling at the ornate script and faded ink. The 15th century illuminated manuscript, an original copy of Sir Thomas Malory's Le Morte d'Arthur, is a priceless treasure.

As I carefully place it back in the climate-controlled vault deep within the library archives, a sense of wistful longing washes over me. What I wouldn't give to step through the pages into the realm of chivalrous knights, powerful sorcerers, and mythical beasts. To escape the tedium of reality, if only for a while.

With a sigh, I seal the vault and make my way back to the polished mahogany circulation desk. The Manhattan Public Library is unusually quiet for a

Monday afternoon. Only the soft swish of pages turning and muted footsteps on thick carpet break the serene hush.

I settle into my chair and absently finger the silver medieval cross pendant at my throat, an heirloom from my grandmother. She's the one who first sparked my fascination with Arthurian legends and tales of Camelot, reading me stories as a girl. I've been enchanted ever since.

The phone rings, jarring me out of my reverie.

"Manhattan Public Library, Aloria speaking. How may I assist you?" I answer automatically.

"Aloria, glad I caught you." It's my co-worker Julia. I'm not exactly sure I would call her a friend, but I suppose she's the closest thing I've got to one. She certainly doesn't understand me at all, but she insists we go out and act like typical girlfriends.

I think she just wants someone to chatter to, and I'm too polite to say no most of the time.

"Are we still on for drinks after work?"

I hesitate, glancing at the stack of returns waiting to be processed. "I'm not sure, Jules. I have a lot to catch up on here."

"Come on, Lori! It's been ages since we had a proper girls' night. You're always holed up in your apartment reading those dusty old history books."

I bristle slightly at her flippant tone. She doesn't understand how alive the past feels to me, how much solace I find in immersing myself in bygone eras.

Still, I know she means well. Perhaps an evening out would do me good. My life has felt stagnant lately, lacking the adventure and enchantment I so often read about.

"Alright, you've convinced me," I relent. "The Raven's Head Tavern at 7?"

"Perfect! See you then. And who knows? Maybe you'll meet a dashing knight in shining armor to sweep you off your feet." Julia gives a conspiratorial laugh before hanging up.

I shake my head ruefully, a wistful smile tugging at my lips. If only real life could be more like the captivating stories of old, full of magic, romance, and world-altering quests.

But real life is mundane, predictable. The only quests I embark upon are tracking down overdue library books. The only magic is in the pages I reverently shelve each day.

As if to punctuate the thought, a patron approaches the desk, a stack of travel guides in hand. I paste on a helpful smile.

"Did you find everything you were looking for?" I ask, scanning the barcodes.

"Yes, thanks," the woman replies distractedly, thumbing at her smartphone. "Just planning a trip to Europe. Trying to decide between London and Paris."

"Both excellent choices. You can't go wrong with either," I say, handing back her books. "Enjoy your travels."

"I will. It'll be nice to get away from reality for a bit, you know?"

I nod in fervent agreement as she walks away. I understand the sentiment all too well.

The rest of the afternoon passes in a blur of task-work—cataloguing new acquisitions, fielding reference questions, preparing for tomorrow's children's story time. Before I know it, the antique grandfather clock in the library foyer is tolling the hour, signaling the end of my shift.

I head out for drinks with Julia.

The Raven's Head Tavern is dimly lit and cozy, with exposed wooden beams and antique kegs stacked behind the bar. The air is thick with the aroma of aged whiskey and wood smoke from the stone fireplace crackling in the corner. It feels like stepping back in time.

Julia waves at me from a booth, her chestnut curls bouncing. "Lori! Over here!"

I slide onto the bench across from her. "This place never changes, does it? I swear it looks exactly the same as when we started coming here after college."

"That's part of its charm," Julia grins, signaling the waiter. "Two pints of the house ale, please."

As we sip the rich, honey-colored brew, Julia chatters on about her latest marketing project and the new guy she's seeing. I try to listen attentively, but my mind keeps wandering to the manuscript I was studying earlier, imagining myself in Queen Guinevere's elegant court gowns.

"Earth to Aloria!" Julia waves a hand in front of my face. "You're doing that thing again. Mentally time-traveling to the Middle Ages. What is your fascination with those times anyway? You realize they didn't take baths or have air conditioners back then, right? They were sweaty and stunk to high heaven." She wrinkles up her nose.

I shrug. "I don't know." How can I explain to her that I've always felt somehow connected to those times? They almost make me feel nostalgic. It doesn't make any sense, I know, but it's how I feel.

So, I say nothing. Instead, I let her chatter on as I dutifully take sips of my drink.

I honestly just can't wait to go home.

Two

My eyelids feel heavy as I sink into the plush mattress, the warmth of the blankets enveloping me like a cocoon. I might have had just a little too much to drink because the darkness sweeps over me, and I drift into a deep slumber almost immediately.

In my dream, a medieval castle looms before me, its stone walls weathered and vine-covered. The air shimmers with an otherworldly luminescence. As if pulled by an invisible string, I float through the castle's winding corridors until I reach a grand chamber.

There, lying upon an ornate four-poster bed draped in silks and velvets, is the most beautiful woman I have ever seen. Her skin is porcelain, her blond hair fanned out around her like a golden halo. She is adorned in an elegant gown of deep crimson, embroidered with gold. Her chest rises and falls with the steady rhythm of eternal slumber.

I move closer, transfixed. "Princess Aveline," I whisper, the name coming to my lips unbidden, as if I have always known it. I reach out a tentative hand to caress her soft cheek. A tingling warmth spreads through my fingertips. Who is she? Why do I feel so drawn to her?

Suddenly, the dream begins to dissipate like mist. I try to cling to it, but it slips through my grasp like water. My eyes flutter open and I lay there, gazing up at my bedroom ceiling, my heart racing. The images of the slumbering princess and the enchanted castle linger in my mind, as tangible as a memory.

I sit up slowly, rubbing my eyes. The dream felt so real, so vivid. An inexplicable longing tugs at my chest, a yearning to return to that place, to the princess's side. I shake my head, trying to clear the cobwebs of sleep.

Throwing off the covers, I pad over to the window and gaze out at the gray dawn. The magical world of my dream has faded, replaced by the dull familiarity of my everyday life. And yet, I can't shake the feeling that something has irrevocably changed within me. That somehow, in the depths of slumber, I brushed against something ancient and mysterious.

I shake my head again. Definitely had waaaay too much to drink last night.

———

The day passes in a haze as I find myself consumed by thoughts of the dream. I lose myself in research, desperate to understand the vivid images that haunt me.

I start with a general search on the medieval period, my eyes scanning through pages about feudal systems, chivalry, and the Crusades.

But it's the castles that capture my attention. I pore over photographs and diagrams, marveling at the intricate stonework, the soaring towers and turrets. I can almost feel the rough stone beneath my fingertips, smell the damp earthiness of ancient mortar.

My search leads me to illuminated manuscripts, their pages adorned with vibrant colors and gleaming gold leaf. I am entranced by the elaborate illustrations of knights and ladies, of mythical beasts and religious iconography. In one image, a beautiful woman lies sleeping, her golden hair splayed across a brocade pillow. The similarity to Princess Aveline sends a shiver down my spine.

As the sun begins to set, casting long shadows across my apartment, I find myself delving into the world of medieval fashion. I study the evolution of gowns, from the simple tunics of the early period to the elaborate houppelandes of the 15th century. I marvel at the rich fabrics—velvet, silk, damask—and the intricate embroidery, the use of precious gems and gold thread. I can almost feel the weight of Princess Aveline's crimson gown, the softness of the velvet beneath my hand.

The more I learn, the more questions arise. Why was Princess Aveline sleeping? Was she enchanted, like the princesses in the fairy tales of my childhood? What secrets lay hidden within the stone walls of that castle?

As night falls, I sit amidst a scatter of books and printouts, my head spinning with information. The dream has consumed me, pulling me into a world long past, a world of magic and mystery. I feel like I'm standing on the precipice of something vast and unknowable, a secret waiting to be uncovered.

Exhausted, I finally crawl into bed, my mind still whirling. As I drift off to sleep, I find myself hoping, with a fervor that surprises me, that I will dream of the castle again. That I will once more stand beside the sleeping princess, will feel that inexplicable connection, that sense of destiny.

And I do.

For the next two weeks, I dream of that medieval castle and the sleeping princess.

Three

The castle looms before me, its stone walls glimmering in the moonlight. An eerie mist swirls around the turrets, beckoning me closer. I shiver, my healer's robes providing little warmth against the chill seeping into my bones. Something feels different this time—a sense of foreboding that causes the hairs on the back of my neck to stand on end.

I step forward, drawn inexplicably toward the heavy oak doors. They creak open at my touch, revealing a cavernous hall bathed in flickering candlelight. My footsteps echo off the marble floor as I make my way deeper inside, following a path I somehow seem to know innately.

At the end of the corridor stands a gilded door, ornate carvings twisting across its surface. I pause, my hand hovering over the handle. Beyond lies the chamber where Princess Aveline slumbers, trapped in an eternal sleep by a wicked curse. I've spent years searching for a cure, scouring ancient texts and experimenting with rare herbs, driven by an inexplicable connection to the princess I've never met.

I take a deep breath and push open the door. Inside, the princess lies on a grand four-poster bed, her golden hair fanned out around her like a halo. She looks peaceful, her delicate features smooth and untroubled, but I know better. The curse holds her in its unyielding grasp, denying her the life she deserves.

As I approach the bed, a sudden gust of wind extinguishes the candles, plunging the room into darkness. The temperature drops, and I wrap my arms around myself, shivering. Something is wrong.

Very wrong.

A sinister laugh echoes through the chamber, and I whirl around, my heart pounding. Standing in the doorway is a figure cloaked in shadows, their face obscured by a deep hood.

"You cannot save her," the figure hisses, their

voice dripping with malice. "The curse is unbreakable. She belongs to me now."

I clench my fists, anger surging through me. "I will never stop trying," I declare, my voice steady despite the fear coursing through my veins. "I will find a way to break the curse and free Princess Aveline."

The figure laughs again, a chilling sound that sends shivers down my spine. "Foolish girl," they sneer. "You have no idea what you're up against. But by all means, keep trying. It will make your inevitable failure all the more delicious."

With that, the figure vanishes, leaving me alone in the dark chamber with the sleeping princess. I turn back to Aveline, my resolve hardening. No matter what dangers lie ahead, I will not rest until I find a way to wake her and restore her to her rightful place. Even if it takes a lifetime.

I reach out and brush a strand of hair from the princess's face, my fingertips grazing her smooth skin. "I will save you," I whisper, my words a solemn vow. "I promise."

Everything blurs as the dream begins to fade...

———

I awake with a start, my body bolting upright in bed. My chest heaves like I've just run a marathon.

The dream...

It was different this time. It was like I was in someone else's body. A healer...searching for a cure to a curse.

The dream lingers in my mind as I try to catch my breath, the details vivid and unsettling.

I've had countless dreams of the sleeping princess before, but never like this. Never from the perspective of someone else, someone so deeply connected to Aveline's plight.

I swing my legs over the side of the bed, my bare feet touching the cool floor. The pre-dawn light filters through the narrow window, casting long shadows across my modest apartment.

I push myself up, my body still trembling from the intensity of the dream.

I move to the small window and look winsomely out it, my brow furrowed.

Something about the dream nags at me, a persistent whisper in the back of my mind. The healer in my dream, the one whose eyes I saw through, whose emotions I felt so deeply...

It felt so real...

I shake my head, trying to clear my thoughts. *It was just a dream*, I tell myself firmly.

Maybe Julia is right.

Maybe I do read too much.

Four

The scent of lavender mingles with the musky aroma of aged parchment as I lean over the weathered tome, my fingertips tracing the inked words that blur before my eyes. Exhaustion weighs heavily on my shoulders, yet sleep eludes me, chased away by the fragments of another life that dance through my dreams.

I pinch the bridge of my nose, willing the visions to fade, but they cling stubbornly like morning mist. Stone walls draped in tapestries, torchlight flickering in drafty corridors, the swish of silk skirts against marble floors—these images haunt me. They seem too vivid to be mere figments of my imagination.

With a sigh, I close the book and tuck it back into its place on the shelf, nestled between other medieval tomes. The familiar scents of the library normally soothe my troubled thoughts, but tonight, even they cannot banish the unease that prickles beneath my skin.

I close up the library and make my way home, where I sink into my soft mattress as I pull the quilt up to my chin.

Maybe tonight will be different. Maybe tonight, I will finally find rest and not dream of *anything*.

But as my eyelids grow heavy and sleep tugs at the edges of my consciousness, I find myself slipping into that other world...

Sunlight streams through the leaded glass windows, warming my face as I blink awake. Disoriented, I sit up, my hands sinking into the plush feather mattress beneath me.

This isn't my bed. These aren't my chambers.

Panic rises in my throat as I take in the opulent surroundings—the intricate tapestries adorning the walls, the gilded mirror reflecting my startled expression, the delicate lace canopy draped above the four-poster bed.

I catch a glimpse of my reflection and freeze.

Golden hair tumbles over my shoulders in shimmering waves, framing a face that is both familiar and foreign. High cheekbones, full lips, and eyes the color of a summer sky stare back at me.

"Princess Aveline, you're awake!" a voice squeaks from the doorway.

I turn to see a young woman in a simple dress, her brown hair pulled back into a neat bun. She is overjoyed, and before I can utter a word, she scurries from the room, calling out loudly. "She's awake! The princess has awakened!"

My heart races as I stare at my unfamiliar hands, slender fingers adorned with glittering rings. This can't be real. I must still be dreaming.

But the cool silk of the nightgown against my skin, the plush carpet beneath my bare feet—it all feels too vivid to be a mere figment of my imagination.

I pinch myself and wince at the sting.

Ow!

Okay, definitely real because you're not supposed to be able to feel physical pain in a dream, right?

I rise from the bed, my legs trembling as I take a tentative step forward.

The door bursts open, and a flurry of activity surrounds me. Maids in crisp uniforms curtsy and fuss over me, their chatter a dizzying buzz in my ears.

"Your Highness, welcome back!" one says with fond tears in her eyes.

"We must prepare you for the day," another one insists, guiding me towards an ornate dressing screen.

I allow myself to be led, my mind reeling as they dress me in layers of silk and lace, cinching my waist with a boned corset that steals my breath.

Is this truly happening? How am I Princess Aveline? Maybe this is just some bizarre, overly vivid dream?

I pinch myself again and wince again.

Nope, not a dream.

Not a dream!

I'm starting to panic.

A knock at the door silences the room. The maids exchange glances before one hurries to answer, her skirts swishing against the polished floor. She curtsies deeply, stepping aside to reveal a tall, broad-shouldered man with piercing blue eyes and a regal bearing.

"Prince Alaric," the maid murmurs, keeping her gaze lowered.

My heart stutters in my chest as recognition

dawns. I have seen this man before, in the fragmented visions that haunt my dreams. But here, in the flesh, he is even more striking—his presence commanding, his gaze intense as it settles upon me.

"Leave us," he commands, his voice rich and deep.

The maids scurry from the room, leaving me alone with the prince. He strides forward, his boots echoing against the stone floor, until he stands before me.

Up close, I can see the fine lines of worry etched into his brow, the shadows beneath his eyes that speak of sleepless nights.

"Aveline," he breathes, his voice softening as he takes my hands in his. "You're awake. Truly awake."

I swallow hard, my throat tight with emotion I cannot name. "I...I don't understand what's happening," I whisper, my voice trembling. "I'm not...I'm not supposed to be here."

His brow furrows, confusion clouding his gaze. "What do you mean? This is your home, your kingdom." He searches my face, his eyes pleading. "Don't you remember?"

I shake my head, tears burning behind my eyes. "I'm not Princess Aveline. My name is Aloria Harding. I'm a librarian from another time, another place. I don't belong here."

The prince's grip tightens on my hands, his expression a mixture of disbelief and desperation. "You're just confused, my dear. You've slumbered for a long while. It might take you a moment to get your bearings back."

I look into his eyes, desperately willing him to understand, but then I swallow and nod slowly.

I don't know myself what's going on here, so how can I expect to explain myself in a way he'll understand? And, I remind myself, I'm in another time period. A time period, that from all my rescarch, was a rather dangerous period in history.

A period when women could be locked up without question.

I probably don't want to come off as too crazy.

I forced a smile. "Yes, you're probably right. Probably just some crazy dream."

Prince Alaric's eyes light up with hope as he takes my hand and threads my arm through his. "I'll help you remember everything. It'll all come back to you. I promise."

He stares at me expectantly when I don't say anything, so I manage another shaky smile.

It looks like I have to pretend to be Princess Aveline. At least for a while.

Until I figure out how the hell to get out of here and back to my real life.

FIVE

The sun-drenched cobblestones feel warm beneath my slippered feet as Prince Alaric guides me through the winding streets of the capital. I try to match his confident stride, smiling and nodding at the enthusiastic faces peering out from doorways and arched windows.

"Princess Aveline! You've awoken at last!" An elderly woman hobbles forward, grasping my hand in her wrinkled fingers. Her rheumy eyes shine with tears. "The gods be praised!"

"Thank you," I murmur, hoping my voice carries the right note of regal warmth. Inside, my heart pounds a staccato rhythm. Will she see through my ruse?

Alaric places a steadying hand at the small of my

back. "Your people have been most anxious for your return." He flashes me a conspiratorial smile before turning to the growing crowd. "The princess still needs rest. We thank you for your prayers and well wishes!"

As he steers me onward, I release a shaky breath. Impersonating a beloved royal is a far cry from my quiet life as Aloria the librarian.

The castle looms ahead, a confection of soaring spires and fluttering pennants. How can I possibly fill Aveline's elegant slippers?

"You used to adore spending time in the glass gardens," Alaric remarks, interrupting my fretting. "Perhaps seeing them will jog your memory."

"I...I'm sure it will help," I agree, remembering to soften the clipped cadence of my commoner's accent.

Inside the domed conservatory, heady floral perfumes wash over me. I inhale deeply, feeling myself relax amidst the nodding blossoms and verdant leaves. At least this much feels familiar.

Alaric plucks a vibrant bloom, tucking it behind my ear with a wistful smile. "Pink astrolilies, your favorite. You would spend hours tending them."

I finger the silky petals, fighting back a wave of misgiving. Aveline's memories remain stubbornly blank, an empty chasm where a lifetime should be.

How long can I maintain this charade before the truth slips free?

"Tell me more about Eldoria's customs," I ask, desperate to fill the silence. "I wish to resume my duties as soon as I am able."

As Alaric regales me with tales of seasonal festivals and court etiquette, I listen intently, each detail a precious key to unlocking Aveline's world. But with every step and story, the weight of my deception grows heavier.

Alaric pauses mid-sentence, his gaze searching mine. "Aveline, are you quite well? You look a bit peaky."

"Just fatigued," I demur, fighting to keep my voice steady. "Perhaps we could continue the tour another time?"

"Of course." He tucks my arm through his as we turn back toward the keep. "We've all the time in the world now that you've returned to us."

If only that were true, I think bleakly. Sooner or later, people will notice the imposter that I am. I might look like her, but I am *not* her. That's for certain.

As we walk in companionable silence, I find myself studying Alaric's profile, the strong lines of his jaw, the way the sun glints off his dark hair. There's a nagging familiarity about him, like a half-remembered dream. Could it be some echo of Aveline's memories, or merely my own fanciful imaginings?

Lost in thought, I stumble over an uneven flagstone. Alaric's hand shoots out to steady me, his grip warm and sure. "Careful, your highness."

For a moment, we stand frozen, his hand lingering on my arm. A peculiar tension hums between us, a sense of recognition that goes beyond mere acquaintance. Alaric's eyes widen, a flicker of hope kindling in their depths.

"Aveline," he breathes, "do you remember...?"

I swallow hard, torn between the desire to reassure him and the knowledge that any false hope I offer will only lead to greater heartbreak. "I...I'm not certain. Everything is still so hazy."

Alaric nods, his expression a mix of disappointment and understanding. "Of course. It will take time." He releases my arm, but the ghost of his touch lingers, sending a shiver down my spine.

As we resume our walk, I can't shake the feeling that there's more to my connection with Alaric than mere duty. But is it truly Aveline's heart that stirs in response to his presence, or my own traitorous feelings, born of loneliness and deceit?

I think back on my solitary existence as a librarian. I used to read romance books and dream of having my very own great love one day.

But this is Princess Aveline's true love—not mine.

I need to remember that.

I push the thought away, focusing instead on memorizing the layout of the keep, the names and faces of the courtiers we pass.

I must be Aveline, fully and completely, if I am to survive in this strange, enchanted world.

But with each step, each shared glance with Alaric, I feel myself slipping further into a web of my own making, where the lines between truth and fantasy blur like mist on a magic-drenched morning.

Six

I stand before the mirror, staring at the reflection that should be my own, but the face looking back at me belongs to Princess Aveline. Her golden hair cascades down my shoulders, her delicate features serene and untroubled.

But deep within, I sense a presence stirring, a whisper of consciousness trapped beneath the surface.

My hands tremble as I press them against the cool glass. "Aveline?" I whisper, my voice echoing in the empty chamber. "Are you there?"

A flicker of movement catches my eye, and for a moment, I swear I see Aveline's lips move, forming silent words. Desperate, I lean closer, my breath fogging the mirror. "Please, if you can hear me, give me a sign."

The room falls still, the only sound the pounding of my own heart. Then, like a distant echo, a voice reaches me, faint but unmistakable. "Help me," it pleads, filled with anguish and desperation. "I'm trapped... the curse..."

Tears sting my eyes as the realization sinks in. Princess Aveline is still here, imprisoned within her own body, cursed to an eternal slumber. The weight of her plea settles heavily upon my shoulders, a burden I never asked for but cannot ignore.

I step back from the mirror, my mind reeling. How can I, Aloria Harding, a mere librarian from another time, break a curse that has held Aveline captive for so long?

But as I gaze at her reflection, I know I cannot turn away.

I must find a way to save her, no matter the cost.

I'm still staring at my reflection—well, Princess Aveline's reflection—when the chamber door creaks open.

I spin around, my heart leaping into my throat. Lady Morgana stands in the doorway, her emerald eyes piercing through me.

I remember the unsettling way the court sorceress's eyes settled on me when Prince Alaric led me through the court earlier that day.

Like she could see right through me.

And apparently, she could.

"You're not her," she states, her voice low and knowing. "You're not Princess Aveline."

Panic grips me, and I stumble back, my words caught in my throat.

I open my mouth to protest, to weave a lie, but something in Lady Morgana's gaze stops me.

There's no accusation there, only a glimmer of understanding.

"I...I'm not," I admit, my voice barely above a whisper. "My name is Aloria Harding. I'm from another time, another place. I don't know how I ended up here, in Aveline's body."

Lady Morgana steps closer, her robes rustling softly. "I sensed a change in Aveline's aura, a different presence within her." She tilts her head, studying me intently. "Tell me, Aloria, what have you discovered?"

I hesitate, unsure if I can trust her. But the weight of my secret is too heavy to bear alone. "Aveline is still here," I confess, my voice trembling. "She's trapped, cursed to sleep forever. I heard her voice, pleading for help."

To my surprise, Lady Morgana nods, her expression grave. "I suspected as much. The curse that holds Aveline is ancient and powerful." She reaches out, placing a gentle hand on my shoulder. "But perhaps your presence here is no accident, Aloria. Perhaps you are the key to breaking the curse and freeing Aveline."

I stare at her, stunned by her words. "Me? But I'm no one special. I don't have magic or power."

Lady Morgana smiles enigmatically. "Magic comes in many forms, my dear. And sometimes, the most unlikely heroes are the ones who change the course of destiny."

She steps back, her gaze lingering on me. "We have much to discuss, Aloria. Together, we may yet unravel the secrets of Aveline's curse and bring her back to us."

I nod, determination filling my heart. "Where do we start?"

Lady Morgana gestures toward the towering bookshelves lining the walls of her study. "We begin with knowledge, Aloria. The curse that binds Aveline is not one I have encountered before, but there may be clues hidden within these ancient tomes."

She moves gracefully, her fingers trailing along the spines of the books. I follow, marveling at the sheer number of volumes, their leather covers worn and cracked with age. The musty scent of parchment and ink fills the air, mingling with the faint aroma of herbs and spices.

As we search, my mind races with questions. Who cursed Aveline? Why would someone do such a thing? And how can I, a mere librarian from another time, possibly hope to break a curse cast by a powerful sorceress?

Lady Morgana seems to sense my doubts. She pauses, turning to face me. "Do not underestimate yourself, Aloria. You possess a keen mind and a compassionate heart. These are weapons as potent as any spell or potion."

Her words bolster my resolve. I nod, my eyes scanning the shelves with renewed purpose. Hours pass as we pour over the books, seeking any mention of curses or sleeping enchantments.

As the candles burn low and the night deepens, a flicker of hope sparks within me. Perhaps, with Lady Morgana's guidance and the knowledge hidden within these ancient tomes, we may yet find a way to free Aveline from her cursed slumber and restore her to her rightful place.

Seven

The sun-dappled leaves crunch beneath our feet as Alaric leads me through the winding pathways of the kingdom. Lady Morgana and I had no luck finding a solution the curse, but she assured me she would keep working on it and that I needed to focus on blending in as best I could for the time being.

So, that's what I'm trying to do as I let Alaric lead me all around the kingdom, trying to spark some memory within me.

Memories I won't have because I'm not Aveline.

His strong hand grasps mine, the warmth of his touch sending sparks tingling up my arm. As we walk, he points out various landmarks—the towering bell tower where he used to hide as a child, the bustling marketplace filled with colorful wares, the ancient stone bridge arching gracefully over the shimmering river.

"Do any of these places seem familiar to you, Aveline?" Alaric asks, his piercing blue eyes searching mine intently. "Do they stir any memories of your life here, before..."

He trails off, not wanting to say the words aloud. Before the curse. Before Aveline became trapped in an endless slumber, her consciousness adrift in a sea of dreams.

I shake my head sadly, golden waves brushing my shoulders. "I'm sorry, Alaric. I wish I could remember something, anything. But it's like peering through a thick fog—shapes and shadows, but nothing clear."

Alaric squeezes my hand reassuringly. "It's alright. We'll keep trying. I know your memories are in there somewhere, just waiting to be unlocked."

We continue on, the gravel path giving way to soft grass dotted with wildflowers. Alaric guides me around a dense thicket of trees, and suddenly we emerge into a hidden garden, a secret oasis tucked away from prying eyes.

My breath catches at the sight. Vibrant blooms in every color imaginable carpet the ground—crimson roses, indigo irises, buttery daffodils, delicate lilac wisteria cascading from latticed arches. In the center stands an ornate fountain, crystal water bubbling merrily over a carved stone basin.

"Oh Alaric," I breathe. "It's beautiful."

A boyish grin tugs at his lips. "I used to come here as a child when I needed to escape the pressures of palace life for a while. To just...be. I always hoped to share it with you someday."

We sit on the edge of the fountain, shoulders brushing. The gentle splash of water and chirping of birds create a melodic background as we drink in the tranquil atmosphere. Alaric plucks a rose from a nearby bush, carefully removing the thorns before tucking it behind my ear with a tender smile.

I find myself captivated by the depths of his ocean eyes, marveling at the genuine care and affection shining there. In this stolen moment, in this enchanted hideaway, it's easy to believe we are simply two hearts entwined by destiny rather than a princess and her betrothed, forever separated by a wicked hex.

If only I could tell him the truth about who I really am—Aloria the librarian, a woman out of time and place. Would he still look at me the same way? Or would I become even more of a stranger to him than Aveline's dormant spirit?

I try to push the thoughts aside and simply savor the magic of the present. The sweet floral fragrance, the warmth of the sun kissing my face, the comforting presence of Alaric at my side.

We sit there for a while before we continue onward.

As we continue our walk through the charming streets of the kingdom, a small, unassuming bookstore catches my eye. Its weathered wooden sign and colorful window display beckon me, promising hidden treasures within.

"Look, Alaric!" I exclaim, pointing to the shop. "A bookstore! Can we go inside?"

Alaric chuckles at my enthusiasm, his eyes crinkling at the corners. "Of course, Aveline. Lead the way."

The bell above the door jingles merrily as we step inside, announcing our arrival. The scent of aged paper and leather envelops us, and I feel an instant sense of homecoming. Rows upon rows of shelves stretch out before us, filled to the brim with ancient tomes and magical tales.

I run my fingers along the spines reverently, marveling at the sheer variety of books. Some are bound in rich, supple leather, while others are encased in delicate, shimmering fabrics that seem to pulse with an otherworldly energy.

"I could spend hours here," I murmur, more to myself than to Alaric.

He smiles, watching me with a mixture of amusement and admiration. "Yes, you've always loved books," he says fondly.

I nod, feeling a blush creep into my cheeks.

We begin to browse the shelves, pulling out volumes that catch our interest. Alaric gravitates towards the history and strategy sections, while I find myself drawn to the tales of magic and adventure.

"Oh, this one looks fascinating!" I exclaim, holding up a book with a shimmering, iridescent cover. "It reminds me of the works of Neil Gaiman. He's one of my favorite authors from the fut-"

I catch myself just in time, realizing my mistake. Alaric tilts his head, confusion etched on his handsome features.

"Neil Gaiman? I've never heard of him. Is he a local author?"

I shake my head, scrambling to cover my blunder. "No, no, never mind. I must have been thinking of someone else."

Alaric seems to accept my explanation, and we continue our exploration of the bookstore. As we chat about our favorite stories and the worlds they conjure, I can't help but feel a pang of longing. If only I could share my true self with him, my passions and experiences from a time he can scarcely imagine.

But for now, I content myself with this shared moment, this connection forged through a love of the written word.

In this cozy haven of books, with Alaric by my side, I can almost forget the weight of my secrets and the uncertain path that lies ahead.

As we step out of the bookstore, the sun hangs low in the sky, painting the kingdom in a warm, golden light. Alaric suggests we find a quiet spot to watch the sunset, and I readily agree, my heart fluttering at the thought of spending more time with him.

We make our way to a grassy hill overlooking the kingdom, the gentle breeze carrying the scent of blooming flowers. Settling down side by side, I can't help but marvel at the beauty of this moment, the peacefulness that seems to envelop us.

Alaric turns to me, his blue eyes shining with

curiosity. "Aveline, it's so wonderful to have you back. You have no idea how much I've missed you."

I pause, my heart constricting in my chest. He thinks I'm someone else. In this moment, with the world bathed in the soft glow of the setting sun, I yearn to share my truth with him. But I know I cannot, not yet.

"It was torture seeing you in that deep sleep and unable to do anything to help you." He shakes his head.

As he speaks, he leans in closer, his hand brushing against mine. Electricity courses through me at his touch, and I find myself drawn to him, our faces mere inches apart.

In this suspended moment, the world seems to fall away. The kingdom, the curse, the secrets that weigh upon my heart, all fade into the background. There is only Alaric and the undeniable connection that pulses between us.

We sit in silence, our eyes locked, our breath mingling in the narrow space that separates us. I can feel the rapid beat of my heart, the longing that threatens to consume me. And in Alaric's gaze, I see a reflection of my own desire, a yearning that transcends the boundaries of time and fate.

The words rise in my throat, burning with the

need to be spoken. I want to tell him everything—who I really am, where I come from, and the inexplicable journey that brought me here. I want to confess the depth of my feelings for him, the way he makes me feel alive and cherished in a way I never thought possible.

But fear holds me back, a cold and unrelenting grip on my heart. What if he doesn't believe me? What if the truth shatters the bond we've forged, the trust we've built? I can't bear the thought of losing him, of watching the warmth in his eyes turn to confusion and betrayal.

So I swallow the words, letting them settle like stones in the pit of my stomach. I'll find the right moment, I tell myself. A time when the truth won't tear us apart, when our love will be strong enough to weather any storm.

Alaric senses my inner turmoil, his brows knitting together in concern. Without a word, he reaches out and takes my hand in his, his touch gentle and reassuring. The simple gesture speaks volumes, a silent promise of understanding and support.

We sit like this for a long moment, our hands entwined, our hearts beating in sync. The sun dips below the horizon, painting the sky in shades of orange and pink, but I barely notice. All I can feel is the warmth of Alaric's skin against mine, the steady strength of his presence beside me.

As the night sky blooms with stars, Alaric begins to share stories from his childhood, his voice soft and wistful. "Do you remember the time we snuck into the kitchens and stole a tray of apple tarts?" he asks, a mischievous glint in his eye. "The cook chased us halfway across the castle grounds before we finally managed to hide in the stables."

I laugh, the sound bubbling up from somewhere deep inside me. "I can only imagine the trouble you must have gotten into," I tease, momentarily forgetting that I'm not the princess he believes me to be.

Alaric grins, his face alight with fond memories. "You were always the mastermind behind our adventures, Aveline. I was just along for the ride."

As he continues to regale me with tales of youthful mischief and carefree days spent exploring the kingdom, I find myself drawn into his world, into the life of the princess I'm pretending to be. For a few precious moments, I allow myself to forget the truth, to bask in the warmth and belonging that Alaric's presence provides.

But even as I lose myself in his stories, my heart aches with the weight of my deception. Each laugh, each shared memory, only serves to deepen the connection between us, making the thought of revealing my true identity even more terrifying.

I long to be honest with him, to lay bare the secrets of my heart and trust in the strength of our bond. Because as insane as it sounds, I *do* feel like I know Alaric. I feel like I've known him forever. Maybe that is just Princess Aveline's feelings coming through me? I don't know.

But the fear of rejection, of shattering this fragile happiness we've found, holds me back.

As the night grows darker and the chill of the evening settles around us, Alaric reluctantly pulls away from our embrace. His eyes search mine, a mixture of concern and tenderness shining in their depths.

"Aveline," he murmurs, his voice low and intimate. "I can sense that something troubles you. Please, know that you can confide in me, no matter what it may be."

I swallow hard, my heart racing at his words. The temptation to pour out my secrets is overwhelming, but I force myself to smile, to shake my head and offer a reassuring squeeze of his hand.

"It's nothing, Alaric. Just the weight of the day catching up with me, I suppose."

He studies me for a long moment, his gaze piercing, as if he can see straight through my flimsy excuse. But he doesn't press, merely nods and offers a soft smile in return.

"Very well. But remember, I am always here for you, Aveline. No matter what."

The sincerity in his words brings tears to my eyes, and I blink them away, not wanting to ruin this perfect moment with my own selfish fears.

"I know, Alaric. And I am grateful for that, more than you could ever know."

We linger there a moment longer, our hands intertwined, our hearts beating in sync. But as the night grows colder and the stars begin to fade, we know it's time to part.

"Until tomorrow, then?" Alaric asks, his voice tinged with a hopeful note.

"Until tomorrow," I echo, my own heart soaring at the thought of seeing him again, even as it aches with the knowledge of what I must eventually do.

We part ways slowly, our eyes locked until the very last moment. As I make my way back to my chambers, my mind is a whirlwind of emotions, my heart torn between the desire to stay and the knowledge that I must eventually find my way home—back to my own time.

But for now, I push those thoughts aside,

focusing instead on the memory of Alaric's embrace, the feel of his hand in mine, and the promise of tomorrow.

And I let myself dream, just for a moment, of a future where we can be together always, free from the curse that threatens to tear us apart.

Eight

The sun dips below the horizon, painting the sky in soft shades of lavender and rose. Prince Alaric and I sit side by side on the stone balcony, our shoulders nearly touching as we gaze out at the tranquil gardens below. The scent of night-blooming jasmine hangs sweetly in the air.

As the days turned into weeks, we've only grown closer, which makes my truth weigh even heavier on my mind.

Because there's no denying it. I am completely in love with Prince Alaric, and that makes me feel terrible because he's taken.

By Princess Aveline.

But enough is enough. It's time I owned up.

I fidget with the embroidered hem of my gown,

my heart racing as I steel myself for what I'm about to say. The weight of my secret presses heavily on my chest, making it hard to breathe. I can't keep deceiving him any longer. He deserves the truth, even if it shatters the fragile bond we've built.

"Alaric," I begin, my voice trembling slightly. "There's something I need to tell you."

He turns to face me, his blue eyes filled with warmth and concern. "What is it, Aveline? You know you can tell me anything."

I take a shaky breath. "That's just it. I'm not Aveline." The words tumble out in a rush before I lose my nerve. "My name is Aloria Harding...and I'm from the future."

Alaric stares at me, his brow furrowed in confusion. "I don't understand. What do you mean, you're from the future?"

I look down at my hands, unable to meet his gaze. "I know it sounds impossible, but it's true. I was born centuries from now, in a world very different from this one. I don't know how or why I ended up here, in Aveline's place. All I know is I started dreaming of this place...her...and then suddenly here I am...in her body. But I swear to you, I'm not her."

A heavy silence stretches between us. When I finally gather the courage to glance up, Alaric is shaking his head slowly. "No, that can't be right. You must be confused, still disoriented from your long sleep. It was just a vivid dream, Aveline. Nothing more."

Desperation claws at my throat. "Please, Alaric, you have to believe me. I'm telling you the truth."

He reaches out and takes my hand, his calloused fingers gentle against my skin. "I know everything must feel strange and uncertain right now. But I promise, whatever dreams may have haunted your slumber, this is your reality. You are Princess Aveline, my betrothed. And I will stand by your side, no matter what comes."

I search his face, seeing only sincerity and unwavering faith in his eyes. He truly believes I am his lost princess, returned to him at last.

The realization settles like a stone in my stomach. How can I convince him of the impossible truth when he so desperately wants to cling to the comforting lie?

I swallow hard, blinking back the tears that sting my eyes. For now, perhaps it's kinder to let him hold onto his illusions. To let him believe that his beloved Aveline has finally awakened, even as my heart aches with the knowledge that I am an imposter in her place.

"Maybe you're right," I whisper, forcing a smile. "It must have been a dream after all."

Alaric's relief is palpable as he pulls me into his embrace, his strong arms encircling me like a protective shield. I can feel the rapid beat of his heart against my cheek, the warmth of his breath stirring my hair.

"I was so afraid I'd lost you forever," he murmurs, his voice thick with emotion. "When you fell into that cursed sleep, it was like all the light had gone out of the world. I searched everywhere for a way to break the spell, but as the years passed, I began to lose hope."

His words pierce my heart like a dagger. The depth of his love for Aveline is clear in every syllable, and the guilt of deceiving him weighs heavily on my soul. But what choice do I have? To shatter his dreams and leave him with nothing but the bitter ashes of disappointment?

I tried to tell him, but he won't believe me.

I cling to him, breathing in the scent of leather and pine that clings to his skin. In this moment, it's easy to pretend that I am the princess he's been waiting for, that the love shining in his eyes is meant for me alone.

But then I'm seized by a sudden anger—not entirely at him but at the unfairness of it all.

I push him back—hard.

I see the shock on his face as I exclaim fiercely, "I'm not her! I'm me! Aloria! Not Aveline!"

Alaric's sudden anger matches my own, startling me. His eyes flash fire before he growls, "I don't care who you are. Aveline, Aloria, it doesn't matter because I love *you*! The woman sitting before me!"

My heart does this weird flutter-flop, but before I can respond, Alaric grabs my face and crashes his mouth onto mine, the heat of his kiss searing me to the core. I melt into him, my doubts and fears momentarily forgotten as I lose myself in the over-whelming tide of sensation.

His kiss isn't the gentle kiss you think of when you think of a typical Prince Charming. It's not sweet and innocent.

It's deliciously dark and sinful and sets my body on fire.

His hands roam over my body, igniting sparks of desire wherever they touch. I arch against him, desperate to be closer, to feel every inch of his skin against mine. The world narrows to the two of us, our gasping breaths and pounding hearts the only sound in the stillness of the night.

We sink down onto the soft grass, the stars wheeling overhead in a glittering canopy. Alaric's eyes are dark with need as he looks at me, his fingers deftly unlacing the ties of my gown. "I want to worship every part of you," he rasps, his voice low and rough with desire. "To show you how much I've longed for this moment."

I nod, beyond words, beyond thought. There will be time enough later for the truth, for the painful reckoning that lies ahead.

But for now, in the sheltering darkness, I will let myself believe in the beautiful lie, and give myself over to the consuming flame of our passion.

His lips fall to my neck, and I feel his hot tongue licking his way down the column of my throat to the swell of my breasts.

My dress falls away, leaving me bare before him. Alaric drinks me in, his gaze scorching a path over my flushed skin. "You're so beautiful," he breathes, reverence and hunger warring in his voice. "I've dreamed of this, of having you in my arms."

His hands skim my sides, calluses rasping deliciously as he maps my curves. I shiver under his touch, sparks of pleasure igniting in my core. Emboldened, I reach for him, tugging impatiently at his clothes until he is as naked as I am.

The heat of his body melds to mine as he settles over me, the hard planes and angles of him fitting perfectly against my softness. I can feel the heavy length of his arousal pressing insistently against my thigh, and a thrill races through me.

"Please," I whimper, not even knowing what I'm begging for, only that I need more, need all of him.

Alaric answers with a deep, claiming kiss that steals the breath from my lungs. His fingers trail lower, teasing over my stomach before dipping between my thighs to the slick, aching place that pulses for his touch.

I cry out as he circles that sensitive bundle of nerves, my hips bucking helplessly into his hand. The pleasure is almost too intense to bear, every stroke winding the coil tighter and tighter within me.

"That's it, my love," Alaric murmurs against my lips. "Let go for me."

His fingers thrust deep, curling just so, and I shatter. Waves of ecstasy crash over me as I come apart, his name a broken litany on my tongue.

Through the haze of aftershocks, I feel him position himself at my entrance. With a fluid roll of his hips, he sheathes himself fully inside my welcoming heat. I gasp at the exquisite stretch, my body accommodating his generous size.

Alaric groans, his face taut with restraint. "Gods, you feel incredible. So tight, so perfect."

He begins to move then, deep, powerful strokes that send jolts of electricity zinging through my veins. I cling to his shoulders, my nails digging into his sweat-slicked skin as he sets a relentless pace. Each thrust pushes me higher, stoking the fire that consumes me from within.

Our bodies tangle together in a primal dance as old as time itself, give and take, advance and retreat. The wet sounds of our joining mingle with the symphony of crickets and the sighing breeze, a sensual melody in the night.

Alaric changes the angle slightly, and suddenly he's hitting that sensitive spot deep inside with every plunge. I keen high in my throat, my legs wrapping around his waist to take him even deeper.

"Yes, right there," I gasp as I throw my head back, lost in the overwhelming sensations as Alaric drives into me again and again, hitting that sweet spot deep inside that makes stars explode behind my eyelids.

The coil of tension in my core winds tighter and tighter, my body trembling on the knife's edge of release.

"Come for me, my princess," Alaric growls

against my neck, his hand snaking between us to rub firm circles over my aching clit. "Let me feel you."

That's all it takes to send me flying. I come with a hoarse cry, my walls clenching around him like a vice as ecstasy crashes through me in relentless waves. Alaric follows me over the edge with a guttural groan, his hips stuttering as he spills his hot seed deep inside me.

We cling to each other as the aftershocks roll through us, chests heaving, hearts pounding in sync. Alaric rains tender kisses over my face, murmuring words of love and devotion against my flushed skin.

In this perfect moment, cocooned in his strong arms under a canopy of stars, everything else fades away. The tangled web of lies, the guilt weighing heavy on my heart, the looming specter of an uncertain future—none of it matters. There is only the two of us, our bodies and souls entwined as one.

Alaric brushes a sweat-dampened curl from my brow, his blue eyes soft and warm as he gazes down at me. "I love you," he says simply, the words ringing with quiet conviction. "No matter what name you bear or what secrets you hold, that will never change."

Tears sting my eyes at the depth of emotion in his voice. I want so desperately to believe him, to trust in the strength of a love that can weather any storm. But a small, insidious voice in the back of my mind whispers that it's all built on a foundation of sand, ready to crumble at the first harsh wind.

What happens when I break the curse? What happens when the real princess Aveline comes back?

I bury my face in the crook of his neck, breathing in his familiar scent as I try to memorize every detail of this precious interlude.

The rasp of his stubble against my cheek, the steady thrum of his pulse beneath my lips, the solid warmth of his body sheltering mine—I etch it all into my memory, a talisman against the uncertain days to come.

For now, I allow myself this stolen moment of peace, this fleeting glimpse of a happiness I fear can never truly be mine. In the morning, I will have to face the consequences of my actions, to grapple with the thorny tangle of my own heart.

But tonight, under the forgiving cloak of darkness, I will savor the sweet illusion of belonging.

Before it shatters.

NINE

The door to my chamber creaks open, revealing Lady Morgana's enigmatic figure, her emerald eyes gleaming with newfound knowledge. "Aloria, I may have uncovered a way to break Princess Aveline's curse," she says, her melodic voice tinged with urgency. "But we must gather the ingredients for a potion."

My heart sinks, a bittersweet ache spreading through my chest. If the curse is broken, my stolen moments with Prince Alaric will vanish like morning mist. Yet, I cannot ignore the call of duty, the need to make things right.

I straighten my shoulders. "What must we do?" I ask, meeting Lady Morgana's gaze with resolve.

"We venture into the heart of the enchanted

forest," she replies, her words laced with cryptic promise. "There, we shall find what we seek."

I grab a cloak. "Lead the way."

As we step into the sylvan realm, the air grows heavy with ancient magic. Gnarled trees whisper secrets, and the earth thrums beneath our feet. I follow Lady Morgana's lithe form, her raven hair cascading down her back like a river of shadows.

Suddenly, a wave of dizziness washes over me. The world tilts, colors bleeding together in a kaleidoscope of confusion. I collapse to the forest floor, my vision fading to black.

In the depths of unconsciousness, a scene unfolds before me. I see Princess Aveline's father, his face etched with sorrow as he turns away from a woman cloaked in darkness. He calls her Lady Blackwood. Her beauty is twisted by bitterness and jealousy.

The scene fades out, and I see Aveline's mother and father holding her as a baby. Their happiness is apparent, but underneath that I feel the rage of the spurned lady.

Lady Blackwood loved the king, but he chose Aveline's mother to be his queen instead.

The scene fades out to another one...Lady Blackwood gifting the golden spinning wheel to the king and queen. They thank her for her kindness.

She grins wickedly, knowing that it's only a matter of time before their daughter gets pricked and her curse is enacted.

Fade out to years later...I'm in Aveline's memory. She's a young woman now, barely eighteen. She stumbles across the spinning wheel. She reaches out.

A single drop of blood blossoms on Aveline's fingertip as the spindle pierces her skin. Her eyes flutter closed, and she crumples to the ground, her golden hair fanning out around her like a halo.

I gasp, jolting awake. Lady Morgana hovers over me, her brow furrowed with concern. "What did you see?" she asks, her voice low and urgent.

I sit up, my head spinning. "It was Lady Blackwood," I whisper, the truth bitter on my tongue. "She cursed Aveline out of jealousy, to punish her father for choosing another as queen."

Lady Morgana nods, her expression grave. "Yes, and the kingdom has been suspended in a frozen state ever since then. None of us have aged since she slumbered," she murmurs, helping me to my feet.

Lady Morgana takes a step back as I stand. "While you were lost in your vision, Aloria, I too was granted a glimpse into the tapestry of fate," she reveals, her voice low and haunting. "It seems that your presence here, in this time and place, is no mere coincidence."

I turn to face her, my heart pounding with a mixture of curiosity and trepidation. "What do you mean?" I ask, searching her enigmatic gaze for answers.

"A magical bond," Lady Morgana breathes, her words hanging in the air like a whispered secret. "I don't fully understand it. It was such a fleeting glimpse, but all I know is that there is an invisible thread that ties your soul to Princess Aveline's. It is this connection that has brought you here, Aloria, to play a pivotal role in her story...and perhaps, in your own."

My mind reels with the implications of her revelation. A bond? With a princess trapped in eternal slumber? The idea seems too fantastical to be true, yet I cannot deny the strange pull I've felt towards Aveline from the moment I first laid eyes upon her sleeping form in my dreams.

And hell, is it any more difficult to believe than I've traveled through time in my dreams?

"I don't understand," I confess, my voice trembling slightly. "What does this bond mean? What am I supposed to do?"

Lady Morgana shakes her head, her expression softening with a touch of sympathy. "The path ahead is shrouded in uncertainty," she admits. "But one thing is clear: your presence here is no accident. You are meant to be a part of this tale, Aloria, for better or for worse."

She reaches into her cloak and retrieves the ingredients she's gathered. "For now, we must focus on the task at hand. The potion," she reminds me, "it may not hold all the answers, but it is a step towards unraveling the curse's hold on Princess Aveline."

I nod. "Let's try it then."

TEN

As the setting sun casts its golden hues across the castle walls, I ascend the stone steps alongside Lady Morgana, our footsteps echoing in the quiet courtyard. My arms ache from carrying the woven basket filled with precious potion ingredients—herbs, roots, and strange vials of shimmering liquids that promise to break Princess Aveline's curse.

"You've done well, Aloria," Lady Morgana says, her voice a melodic whisper. "With these components, I believe we have all we need to concoct the elixir."

I nod, my heart fluttering with a mix of hope and trepidation. "Will it truly work? Can we really save the princess and return me to my own time?"

Lady Morgana's emerald eyes meet mine. "We can only hope," she says frankly. "Come, let us begin."

We enter Lady Morgana's chamber, a room filled with the heady aroma of incense and the soft glow of candles. I watch as she methodically arranges the ingredients on a weathered wooden table, her slender fingers deftly measuring and mixing with practiced ease.

Minutes stretch into hours as Lady Morgana works, her brow furrowed in concentration. I pace the room, my mind whirling with thoughts of home, of the life I left behind.

Granted, it wasn't much of a life, I suppose. I don't have any family or friends to speak of. I was just a simple, quiet librarian.

But still, it was *my* life.

Somehow, though, the thought of never returning there doesn't hurt as much as it used to.

The thought of leaving here—leaving *him*—is what hurts.

At last, Lady Morgana holds up a small vial, the liquid within shimmering like starlight. "It is done," she declares, her voice tinged with triumph.

I take the vial with trembling hands, my heart

pounding in my chest. This is it—the moment of truth.

In just a moment I could be back in the future.

My heart falls. I might never see Prince Alaric again.

But Princess Aveline will be free.

It's the right thing to do.

Tears prick my eyes.

I raise the elixir to my lips and swallow, the liquid cool and faintly sweet on my tongue.

Nothing happens.

I wait, holding my breath, but there is no rush of magic, no swirling vortex to carry me back to my time. Instead, a wave of exhaustion washes over me, my limbs growing heavy as lead.

"Lady Morgana, what's happening?" I whisper, my words slurring as I sway on my feet.

She catches me as I crumple, lowering me gently to a plush velvet chaise. "Sleep now, Aloria," she murmurs, her voice distant and echoing. "Rest, and let the magic take its course."

My eyelids flutter shut, and I slip into a deep, dreamless slumber. But even in the darkness of my unconscious mind, despair takes hold. Tears stream down my face as the realization sinks in—I am trapped, forever bound in this sleep.

I just know it.

In my mind's eye, I see the face of Prince Alaric, fading like mist in the morning sun. I reach for him, but he slips away, leaving me alone in the void.

A sob tears from my throat, the sound of a heart breaking, of hope shattering like glass.

I am lost, adrift in a sea of sorrow, with no way back to the life I once knew.

And as the darkness consumes me, I can only wonder: will I ever find my way home again?

Eleven

I stand before the ethereal pond, its surface shimmering with an otherworldly glow.

My heart races as I grip the vial containing the potion that will break the curse and save the kingdom, but at the cost of sending me back to my own time, forever separating me from Alaric.

I don't even know where it came from or how it got into my hands. I don't know how I got here.

But here I stand on the precipice of a choice that will change my life forever.

Aveline's life.

The lives of all the people in the kingdome of Eldoria, forever frozen in time.

I know what I have to do.

Here in my subconscious I have to make the choice to sacrifice myself—my love for Prince Alaric—to save Princess Aveline and the entire kingdom.

I don't know how I know this. Just that I do.

So, here goes...

Tears blur my vision as I uncork the vial with trembling hands. I lift my gaze to see Alaric standing on the other side of the pond, his handsome face etched with sorrow and longing. Our eyes meet, a thousand unspoken words passing between us.

As the potion touches my lips, a blinding light engulfs me. Pain sears through my body as the curse unravels, ancient magic swirling around me in a dizzying vortex. I cry out, my consciousness fracturing...

And then, clarity. Memories flood my mind—memories of a life lived as Princess Aveline. Lavish banquets in the palace, horseback rides through sun-dappled forests with Alaric by my side, the weight of a crown upon my head. The curse had sent me forward in time, into the body of my future self, Aloria.

I blink, disoriented, as the light fades. I am no longer standing by the pond. I awaken in my bed, Princess Aloria's bed, for I am indeed she.

I am no longer Aloria the librarian, but Princess Aveline, returned to my rightful place.

Alaric is by my side, his eyes red from tears but now wide with joy and shock. "Aveline? Is it really you?"

"Yes, my love," I whisper, a radiant smile spreading across my face as I take his hands in mine. "I remember everything now. The curse, it sent me to the future, to live as Aloria until I could find my way back to you."

He pulls me into a tight embrace, his strong arms enveloping me. I breathe in his familiar scent, feeling the steady beat of his heart against my cheek. Around us, the kingdom stirs to life, freed from the oppressive curse at last.

Tears of relief and joy stream down Alaric's face as he cups my cheek, his touch gentle and reverent. "When Lady Morgana told me of your sacrifice, of how your love for me and your selflessness freed the kingdom, I could scarcely believe it. I thought I'd lost you." His voice breaks as he brings my hand to his lips to kiss it reverently.

I lean into his touch, savoring the warmth of his skin against mine. "In my heart, I always knew that our love would conquer any obstacle. Even when I lived as Aloria, a part of me yearned for you, for the life we were meant to share."

Alaric's eyes shine with admiration and gratitude. "You were so brave, Aveline. You really didn't know who you were, yet you were willing to give up your chance of returning home, to endure the heartbreak of seeing me with another...I cannot imagine the strength that must have taken."

I shake my head, a soft smile playing on my lips. "It was not strength, but love that guided me. I would have done anything to save you, to save our people. And in the end, it was that love that set us all free."

He takes my hand, pressing a fervent kiss to my palm. "And now, we have a second chance. A chance to build the life we always dreamed of, to rule this kingdom together."

As I gaze into his eyes, I see a future filled with hope and possibility. "I love you, Alaric."

"And I love you Aveline, my brave princess. Always."

In this moment, surrounded by the warmth of Alaric's love and the promise of a new beginning, I feel truly alive. The curse that once defined my existence is now nothing more than a distant memory.

Our love was strong enough to transcend time itself.

Alaric kisses me, and I finally know that I am exactly where I am meant to be—in the arms of my true love.

For I *am* Princess Aveline.

Twelve

Sunlight streams through the stained glass windows of the throne room, bathing the marble floor in a kaleidoscope of colors.

I stand hand in hand with Alaric before the cheering crowd, their joyous cries echoing off the high ceilings. My heart swells with love and gratitude as I look out at the faces of our people—the lines of worry and hardship erased, replaced by hope and happiness. We have come so far.

Alaric squeezes my hand and I turn to face him, drowning in the ocean of his blue eyes. "You were born to wear that crown, my love," he murmurs. "The kingdom is blessed to have you as their queen."

"Only because I have you by my side, my king," I

whisper back. Emotion clogs my throat. To think we almost lost this, lost each other...

The celebration goes on for hours, but I'm only half aware, my mind adrift with memories of our journey here. The curse, the quest, the seemingly insurmountable obstacles we overcame together. And now, a new adventure stretches before us— ruling a kingdom, rebuilding a land, starting a family.

It's daunting and thrilling all at once.

When the last reveler finally departs, Alaric pulls me into his strong arms. "I thought this day would never come," he says hoarsely. "That I'd never get to hold you again."

Tears spring to my eyes. "You never gave up on me, even when all seemed lost. Your love saved me."

He kisses me then, deeply, urgently. I melt into him, the rest of the world falling away until all that exists is the press of his body against mine.

He lifts me up and strides purposefully towards our bedchamber, kicking the door shut behind us.

Clothing is shed hastily between searing kisses, hands roaming over heated skin. He lays me down on the bed, worshipping every inch of my body until I'm trembling with need.

When his hot mouth finds my nipple, I arch up into his, wetness flooding between my thighs.

"So wet for me already, my queen," Alaric rasps, his fingers delving into my slick folds. "I need to taste you."

He kisses a fiery trail down my body until his head is buried between my legs. The first stroke of his tongue against my aching sex tears a cry from my lips.

Gripping his hair, I grind myself shamelessly against his face as he laps and sucks at my throbbing clit.

"Alaric, please," I whimper, my hips bucking wildly. "I need you inside me."

Rising over me, he notches his rock hard cock at my entrance. "I love you, Aveline," he breathes. "Now and forever."

"And I love you," I whisper back.

With a powerful thrust, he sheaths himself to the hilt in my tight heat. I moan loudly, my walls stretching to accommodate his impressive size. He sets a driving rhythm, plunging deep before withdrawing almost all the way, stoking the fires climbing higher and higher.

Our bodies move together in perfect synchronicity, slick with sweat, lost to sensation. Nothing else matters except this.

Our love.

He drives harder and faster, kissing me all the while until I shatter in his arms, pleasure crashing over me in waves. He follows a moment later, my name a reverent prayer on his lips.

We lay tangled together afterwards, sweat-slicked and sated, trading soft kisses and words of adoration.

As I drift off to sleep, secure in Alaric's embrace, a profound sense of peace washes over me.

The lost princess and her devoted prince, finally home.

And they lived happily ever after, indeed.

Don't miss the rest of the Spicy Romantasy series! Go to www.authorkenzieskye.com to find out where to get the rest of the series and to get a free book!